# JAMES STEVENSON

# CHRISTMAS
## AT MUD FLAT

Greenwillow Books
*An Imprint of HarperCollinsPublishers*

For Sidney and Avodah

Watercolor paints and a black pen were used
to prepare the full-color art.
The text type is Della Robbia.

Christmas at Mud Flat
Copyright © 2000 by James Stevenson
All rights reserved.
Printed in Singapore by Tien Wah Press.
www.harperchildrens.com

Library of Congress Cataloging-in-Publication Data

Stevenson, James, (date)
Christmas at Mud Flat / by James Stevenson
    p.    cm.
"Greenwillow Books."
Summary: The animal residents of Mud Flat go about
their preparations for Christmas in their own ways.
ISBN 0-688-17301-2 (trade).
ISBN 0-688-17302-0 (lib. bdg.)
[1. Animals—Fiction. 2. Christmas—Fiction.] I. Title.
PZ7.S84748 Ch 2000    [E]—dc21    99-025064

1 2 3 4 5 6 7 8 9 10    First Edition

# Contents

1. Who's Going to Be Santa? · · · 4

2. Sheldon's List · · · 8

3. Freddie's Fix-It Shop · · · 10

4. Prudence Is Choosy · · · 16

5. Sherwood Plans Ahead · · · 20

6. Sky Watch · · · 28

7. Cookies · · · 34

8. The Christmas Eve Party · · · 36

9. Christmas Eve · · · 40

# 1

## Who's Going to Be Santa?

It was the week before Christmas,
and everybody in Mud Flat
was trying to get ready.

"Who's going to dress up as Santa Claus
for the Mud Flat party this year?"
said Hodges.
"I guess it will be Marshall again,"
said Arthur.
"As usual."
"Why is it always Marshall?" said Elsie.
"Yes, why?" said Priscilla.
"Because he looks like Santa," said Arthur.
"Big and fat and jolly."

"How do you know Santa looks
like that?" said Hodges.

"Everybody knows," said Arthur.

"Have you ever seen him?" said Brian.

"Or her?" said Elsie.

"Well, no," said Arthur. "I haven't."

"Do you know anybody who has?"
said Brian.

"Not in Mud Flat, no," said Arthur.

"They may have seen him over in
Fog Hollow or Crescent Beach."

"Maybe he's not as big or as fat or
as jolly as you think," said Hodges.
"You could be right," said Arthur.
"It doesn't *have* to be Marshall."
"No, it doesn't," said Elsie. "This
year let's have somebody else."
"Okay with me," said Arthur.
"But who?"
"We'll just have to look around,"
said Hodges, "and see who
would be good."

# 2

## Sheldon's List

"What are you writing?" said Eunice.

"My Christmas list," said Sheldon.

"Kind of long, isn't it?" said Eunice.

"I figure it can't hurt," said Sheldon.

"What are you asking for?" said Eunice.
"Pretty much the same stuff I asked for
last year," said Sheldon. "A bicycle,
a baseball glove, a kite, a sled, a pool table,
a canoe, a guitar, a train ride, a piano,
and a pair of socks."
"What did you get?" said Eunice.
Sheldon took off his shoes.

"Like 'em?" he said.
"Gorgeous," said Eunice.

# 3

## Freddie's Fix-It Shop

Freddie was very busy in his fix-it shop
down by the pond.

"Freddie," said Roy, "could you fix up
this toy wagon in time for Christmas?
My grandson would love it."

"I could try," said Freddie.

"Thanks, Freddie," said Roy.

Roy went out, and Maria came in.

"I know you're busy, Freddie," said Maria,

"but do you think you'd have time to put

a new top on this drum?"

"Probably," said Freddie.

"Before Christmas, I mean," said Maria.

"I know," said Freddie.

Maria left, and one end of a sofa
came bumping through the door.

"We're having lots of relatives for
Christmas dinner, Freddie," said Mischa.
"We need to use this sofa," said Nancy.
"Looks like it needs a new leg,"
said Freddie.
"Exactly!" said Mischa.
"I'll see what I can do," said Freddie.

"Any chance you could get my bass
in shape for Christmas Eve, Freddie?"
said Murray. "We want to have
music at the big party."
"Lean it over
there, Murray,"
said Freddie.
"I'll take a look at it
as soon as I can."

"Thanks, Freddie," said Murray.
"I hope you'll be coming to the party!"
"Probably not," said Freddie.
"Once I get my work done,
   I usually fly south on Christmas Eve."

"See you later," said Murray.
"I have a lot to do."
He went out.
Freddie sat down on the
broken sofa and gave a sigh.

# 4

## Prudence Is Choosy

Grover and Leonard were
pushing their way through the snow.
"I would like to find a good present
for Prudence this year,"
said Grover. "But what?"

"Prudence is choosy," said Leonard.

"You said it," said Grover. "Last year
   I gave her a leaf the color of a pumpkin.
   It was beautiful!"

"Did she like it?" said Leonard.

"I don't think so," said Grover. "She left
   it behind at the Christmas party."

"Well, good luck," said Leonard.
   He turned off. "I have to wrap some
   presents myself."

"See you later, Leonard," said Grover.
   Grover pushed on into the woods.
   He saw a fallen birch tree.

"Birch bark!" said Grover. "White and dusty
   with little black stripes—I love it!"

He pulled off a loose piece. "You can't beat birch bark," he said. "What a great Christmas present!"
He carried the birch bark out of the woods.

Grover was coming around a rock when he bumped into Prudence.
"Hello, Grover," said Prudence. "What have you got there?"
"Birch bark," said Grover.
"You must be going to make a nice fire in your fireplace," said Prudence.
"Not exactly," said Grover.
"Well, keep warm," said Prudence.

Grover was almost home when he
saw Estella. She was making a snowman.
"Nice snowman, Estella," said Grover.
"Thanks, Grover," said Estella. "Where
did you ever find that beautiful birch bark?"
"In the woods," said Grover.
"It would make a swell Christmas present
for somebody," said Estella.
"I believe you're right," said Grover.
"And I think I know who."

# 5

## Sherwood Plans Ahead

Sherwood took his morning tea out
onto the porch.

Mrs. Tompkins came rushing by,
carrying packages.

"Good morning, Mrs. Tompkins," said
Sherwood. "Enjoying the holiday season?"
"I am frantic," said Mrs. Tompkins. "Only
one week left, and so much to do!"
Sherwood took a sip of tea.
"There is no reason to get all worked
up about Christmas, if you plan ahead,"
said Sherwood. "That's what *I* do."
"Good for you, Sherwood," said
Mrs. Tompkins, and hurried away.

"Now I shall wrap my presents,"
said Sherwood. "Right on schedule."
He went upstairs to his room.

"Everything is in order," he said, looking at his table. "I have the handsome green wrapping paper. I have the scissors. I have the lovely brand-new roll of red ribbon."

Sherwood took the scissors and carefully cut a piece of wrapping paper. In the middle he put his present for Cousin Fauntleroy—a framed picture of Mud Flat at sunset—and folded the green paper around it. He put his finger on top to hold it in place.

"Now for a bit of ribbon," he said.

Sherwood reached for the roll of
ribbon and knocked it off the table.
"Oh, dear!" cried Sherwood.

He grabbed the end of the ribbon,
but the roll went bouncing across
the floor and out the door.

It went down the stairs.
"Stop!" cried Sherwood.

It rolled out the front door, across
the porch, and down the steps.
Sherwood ran after it.

The ribbon slipped out of his hand and
went slithering away across the snow.
"Are you looking for a red ribbon?"
said Pendleton. "It went that way."
"Thank you, Pendleton," said Sherwood.
"I see it."

The ribbon went faster and faster.
It went up the
side of a tree,
and over
a branch,
and down
again.

Sherwood ran as fast as he could,
but he couldn't catch up.
The ribbon hit a rock, bounced into
the air, and landed in the back of
Victor's pickup truck.

Victor drove away.
"Where is Victor going?" said Sherwood.
"He said he was going to visit his grandchildren
  for Christmas," said Woerner.

"There goes my red ribbon,"
  said Sherwood.
"You don't have any more?"
  said Woerner.
"No, I don't!" said Sherwood.

"Take my advice, Sherwood,"
  said Woerner. "Next Christmas,
  plan ahead."

# 6

## Sky Watch

It was Christmas Eve.

Larry and Albert were sitting in their
tree house, listening to the sounds of
the party.

Moira passed by down below. "What
are you doing up there?" she called.
"It's time for the party."

"We're keeping our eyes out for Santa
   Claus," said Larry. "We want to make sure
   he doesn't miss Mud Flat in the dark."
"If he goes overhead,"said Albert,
"I'm going to blow my bugle."
"And I'm going to yell," said Larry.
"Good idea," said Moira. "But it must
   be cold up there."
"It is," said Larry. "But somebody
   has to do it."

"It wouldn't be so bad if we had
a little hot chocolate," said Albert.
"And maybe a couple of cookies,"
said Larry. "Raisin, if possible."
"I'll see what I can do," said Moira.
"The faster the better, Moira!" said Albert.
Moira hurried off.

"Katchoo!" said Larry a little later.
"I could be catching a cold!"
"Where is Moira and the hot
chocolate?" said Albert. "I'm freezing."
"Maybe she forgot," said Larry.
"I think I'll go see," said Albert.
"Me, too," said Larry.
"We could save her a trip," said Albert.

"But who's going to watch for
Santa Claus?" said Larry.
"We can watch from different
windows at the party," said Albert.
"Good idea!" said Larry.
They climbed down from
the tree house and
hurried to the party.

A few minutes later Moira came along
carrying a tray. On it were three cups,
a pot of hot chocolate, and a plate
of raisin cookies.

Moira started to climb up to the tree house.
"Here you are!" she called.

The tray tilted, and the cookies slid off.
Moira kept climbing.
The tray tipped
the other way,
and the cups
fell off.

By the time Moira got to the top,
the hot chocolate was gone, too,
fallen onto the snow.

"Albert?" said Moira. "Larry?"
Moira sat down.
"I guess it's up to me to watch for
Santa," she said. "But what do I do
if I see him?" she said. "I don't even
have a bugle."

She began to shiver. "I guess I might
as well go to the party," she said, and
climbed down from the tree.

# 7

## Cookies

Kevin and Armand were walking
under the tree house when
Kevin suddenly stopped.

"Armand," he whispered. "You won't
believe this!"

"What is it?" said Armand.

"Cookies in the snow," said Kevin.

"How can that be?" said Armand.

"Strange and wonderful things happen
on Christmas," said Kevin, "like cookies
in the snow."

He took a bite. "Mmm," he said.

"Mmm," said Armand.

# 8

## The Christmas Eve Party

Maria played the drum that Freddie
had fixed, and Murray played the bass,
and lots of people danced.

"Where's Santa Claus tonight?"
said Lauren.
"I don't know," said Marshall.
"This year it isn't me."

"I wonder who it is?"said Lauren.
"Here's Santa now!" cried Elsie.
Everybody turned to look.
"Where?" said Clifton.
"I don't see him," said Ruth.

"Ho, ho, ho," said a small voice.

"There he is!" said Vernon. "Down there!"

They all looked where Vernon was pointing.

"It's Priscilla!" whispered Mrs. Tompkins.

"Welcome, Santa!" said Roy.

"Merry Christmas! Ho, ho, ho!"
said Priscilla.

"Nice outfit, Santa!" said Enid.

"I'm not really Santa Claus," said Priscilla.
"This is a costume."

"You could have fooled me!" said Enid.

"You *did* fool me!" said Marshall.

"Ho, ho, ho," said Priscilla.

"How about a cup of cider?" said Lewis.

"I believe I will," said Priscilla.

"Being Santa is hot work!"

# 9

## Christmas Eve

It was nearly midnight in Mud Flat.
The party was over. Everybody had gone
to bed, but not everybody was asleep.
Cadwell felt a breeze coming through
the window. He heard a sound like chimes.

Nell heard the same sound.
She got up and looked
out the window.

Clem and Doak looked out their window, too.
"Where did that music come from?"
said Clem.
"I have no idea,"
said Doak,
"but I don't hear
it anymore."

"What do you see, Percy?" said Enid.

"Just a dark, dark night," said Percy.

"Those chimes were probably just a dream," said Cadwell. "It's back to bed for me."

Then there was a gust of wind, and
everybody in Mud Flat heard the chimes.
They all got up to look.
Some put on coats or bathrobes and stood
on their porches, listening to the soft music
coming on the wind.

Then the moon came out from behind
a cloud, and suddenly everybody
could see the big tree next to the
pond sparkling in the moonlight.

"Who put all those ornaments on the tree?" said Cadwell.

"Somebody very tall," said Sherwood.

"Or somebody good at climbing," said Enid.

"Or flying," said Percy.

Clem and Doak ran to the tree to take a closer look.

"It's not regular ornaments!" said Clem.

"It's bottle caps and tin cans and nails and screws and all kinds of junk!" said Doak.

"Freddie!" said Eunice. "He's the only one
who would have that stuff."
"Of course," said Sheldon. "It's a present
from Freddie!"

"Where is he?" said Cadwell. "We should
thank him."
"Freddie always flies south on Christmas
Eve," said Patrick. "He's long gone by now."
They watched the tree glittering and listened
to the music, until at last the clouds moved in
across the moon, and Mud Flat was dark again.

Everybody went back to bed.

An hour later Cadwell woke up.

"Sleigh bells," he said.

He went to the window.

Everybody was looking out.

"Did you hear them?" he asked.

"Right over my roof."

"Mine, too," said Eunice.

"Better get some shut-eye," said Enid.

"Tomorrow is a big one."

"It's already tomorrow," said Cadwell,
  looking at his pocket watch.
"In that case," said Mrs. Winkleham,
  "Merry Christmas, everybody!"
"Merry Christmas!" called the others,
  and a few minutes later Mud Flat
  was sound asleep.